The Hammer

PRAISE FOR *STORYSHARES*

"One of the brightest innovators and game-changers in the education industry."
– Forbes

"Your success in applying research-validated practices to promote literacy serves as a valuable model for other organizations seeking to create evidence-based literacy programs."

- Library of Congress

"We need powerful social and educational innovation, and Storyshares is breaking new ground. The organization addresses critical problems facing our students and teachers. I am excited about the strategies it brings to the collective work of making sure every student has an equal chance in life."
– Teach For America

"Around the world, this is one of the up-and-coming trailblazers changing the landscape of literacy and education."
- International Literacy Association

"It's the perfect idea. There's really nothing like this. I mean wow, this will be a wonderful experience for young people."   - Andrea Davis Pinkney, Executive Director, Scholastic

"Reading for meaning opens opportunities for a lifetime of learning. Providing emerging readers with engaging texts that are designed to offer both challenges and support for each individual will improve their lives for years to come. Storyshares is a wonderful start."
- David Rose, Co-founder of CAST & UDL

The Hammer

Devan Hawkins

STORYSHARES

Story Share, Inc.
New York. Boston. Philadelphia

Published in the United States by Story Share, Inc.

The characters and events in this book are fictitious. Any similarity to real persons, living or dead, is entirely coincidental.

Storyshares
Story Share, Inc.
24 N. Bryn Mawr Avenue #340
Bryn Mawr, PA 19010-3304
www.storyshares.org

Inspiring reading with a new kind of book.

Interest Level: Middle School
Grade Level Equivalent: 3.5

9781642615012

Book design by Storyshares

Printed in the United States of America

Storyshares Presents

1

The sounds from the hammer shook the boy awake. They came in bursts of four rhythmic strikes. A brief silence would linger after the last strike. Then a new sequence would begin.

The boy stared at the ceiling. He wanted to sleep longer, but the beating of his dad's hammer and the humid air made it impossible. Instead, he sat up and crawled to the bottom of his bed. He stared out the window.

His father was crouched on the roof of the shed he was building in their front yard, laying shingles. Yesterday his dad had said that once the roof was done, all the shed needed was windows and paint.

Pretty soon, the boy knew he would hear his father's voice from outside telling him to help. To bring extra shingles from underneath the deck or grab a tape measurer from the basement. Ever since he'd been laid off a few months earlier, his father had thrown himself into any task he could find around the house. As a result, the boy had spent most of his summer helping his father. Together they dug post holes for a new fence, replaced the lattice work on the deck, and now the shed.

2

The boy looked through the trees behind the shed where he could see Tyler's house. Tyler was a year older than him. They had met the summer before, in the trees between their houses. The boy's older sister had taken him into the trees to see a fort that Tyler had built with his own sister. The fort was made of fallen branches. Tyler had set the branches upright in a circle to make a teepee. The section facing Tyler's house had an opening, so they could all go inside of it.

The boy had been ready to argue if Tyler said he couldn't go into the fort. But Tyler said they could play in there whenever they wanted. He called the area between their houses "no man's land."

Tyler went to a private Catholic school. So, he didn't wait for the bus with the other kids from down the street. But the boy would see Tyler on weekends.

3

One day, the boy and Tyler were in the fort together. Tyler had to leave because he had to go with his mother to her doctor's appointment. Later, the boy's mom told him that Tyler's mom had cancer. The boy and Tyler still played on weekends, but Tyler never said anything about his mom.

The boy thought little about Tyler's mom until last week. He had been sitting on the computer in his parents' room, playing a video game. His mom came in and asked him to stop playing for a minute. She sat on the bed across from him. She said that Tyler's mom would likely pass away soon.

The boy couldn't understand what his mom meant. No one ever said that Tyler's mom was dying, only that she was sick. What did that even mean? He knew she had recently returned home after spending months in the hospital. But the boy thought that was because she was feeling better. He thought it meant that the cancer was going away. His mom hugged him when he started to cry.

The last time the boy had seen Tyler was a week ago. One of their neighbors had set up a rotation where families in the neighborhood would bring meals to Tyler's family. The boy had gone over with his Cub Scout den to drop off a baked chicken dinner his mom had made. It was the first time he had seen Tyler in a few weeks. The boy told Tyler that he had just gotten a rare Pokémon card. After the boy got home, his mom told him that he shouldn't have told Tyler about the card.

4

At night, the boy tried to imagine what it looked like inside Tyler's house. Was his mom hooked up to a machine that beeped all night? Were they standing around her all the time, waiting? Did Tyler read about the disease online and dream about miracle cures? It was hard for the boy to believe that right next door, someone's life was about to end. But inside his house, everything was normal.

The boy heard his dad's hammer stop. He knew what was coming.

"Are you awake? Come out here." His dad's voice echoed like the hammer strikes.

The boy rolled off the bed and walked downstairs. He could feel the heat coming through the screen door before he opened it. It was bright outside. His eyes were almost shut as he walked over to the shed.

"Why aren't you wearing any shoes?"

His dad was staring down at him from the top of the shed. The boy looked at his feet. He never liked to wear shoes in the summer. He preferred the heat of the driveway's asphalt to the suffocating heat of his shoes.

"If you're gonna help me, you need to wear shoes."

The boy turned and walked back into the house without saying anything.

"While you're inside, can you go down to the cellar and grab the electric sander?" his dad shouted as the boy slid his shoes on without socks.

5

The boy knew the sander was in the corner near the furnace, but he didn't go to it right away. He loved the cellar, especially on hot days. Earlier in the week, he had asked his mom if he could sleep down there. He had his radio ready. He wanted to lie down in his sleeping bag and listen to the Red Sox play the Devil Rays, but she said no.

Even in the corner with the furnace, furthest away from the shed, he could hear the echo of his dad's hammer. He wondered whether Tyler's family could hear it, too.

Of course they could hear it, he realized. It was so hot out that their windows must be open. What did Tyler think about his dad hammering away all morning while Tyler's mom lay in her bed dying? What if she was trying to say something to her kids and each word was cut off by the sounds of the hammer? What if they just wanted to rest and the hammer was keeping them awake?

The sander was heavy when the boy finally picked it up. He held it with both hands. When he reached the shed, his dad climbed down.

"You know about Tyler's mom?" the boy asked his dad as he took a sip of pink lemonade.

"Yeah, your mother told me. It's really sad."

The boy had more that he wanted to say, but he didn't know how to say it. He plugged the orange extension cord into the sander. But it didn't turn on when his dad flicked the switch.

"Goddamnit," the boy's dad grumbled. "Go check if the cord fell out of the socket."

The boy walked toward the socket at the side of the house. He didn't know how he could bring up the hammering to his dad. Working on the shed was practically all he ever did. The boy knew his dad wouldn't spend a day sitting around.

6

A few days earlier, his dad said that he would have been done with the shed if they hadn't gotten so much rain when he was building the foundation. The boy was afraid that if he said anything, his dad would think he was just lazy.

The boy's mom would be home from the bank soon. Maybe he could mention the disruptive hammering to her. She would know how to tell his dad about it. She understood. She was the one who told him about Tyler's mom anyway.

But how long would it be until she was home? How many times would that hammer echo off the side of Tyler's house before the boy's mom said something about it? Would Tyler's mom already be dead?

The orange extension cord was on the ground. The boy thought about telling his dad the sander was plugged in and that it must be broken. He wondered how long it would take his dad to realize he was lying. He wondered if that delay would give Tyler and his family any relief.

The boy reached down and plugged in the cord.

His dad climbed back up to the roof with the sander. When he turned it on, the sound was even louder than the hammer had been. There was no break from it. It didn't fade and return like the hammer. It was steady and loud. In fact, it felt like it kept getting louder.

7

The boy put his hands over his ears. "Dad! Dad!" he yelled as loud as he could. But his dad kept sanding. It was five minutes before he turned it off.

"Were you saying something?" his dad asked.

"That thing is so loud," the boy said.

"Sure it is. Would you rather we sand the whole thing by hand?"

"No—I just thought that it might bother Tyler's family."

His dad paused for a moment. "I don't think it's that loud. They can probably barely hear it inside. I'm almost done anyway."

His dad started the sander again. The boy's hands returned to his ears.

He started to cry. His dad didn't get it. Tyler's mom was dying, and there was nothing he could do about it. The least they could do was not make things worse.

Why did it matter if it took another day to finish the damn shed? The boy thought about following the orange cord back to the sander and unplugging it, but he knew that wouldn't make a difference. Pretty soon the sanding would be done. Then his dad would go back to hammering.

The boy knew he couldn't keep thinking about it. He distracted himself by thinking about the Red Sox's batting lineup. He tried to remember each player's number of home runs and their batting average.

It was an afternoon filled with more sanding and more hammering before the boy's mom got home. He hoped she would have some news about Tyler's mom.

8

"Do you know anything?" he asked her after she got out of her car and kissed his forehead. She knew exactly what he was talking about.

"I haven't heard a thing. I don't even know who would tell me. It's better to just let them be right now."

"Do you think you could call them and ask?" The boy knew that was a bad idea even as he asked the question. His mom just shook her head.

The boy didn't want to bother them. But how could they not be bothered by all the loud hammering, sanding, and electric screwdriving?

"I'm afraid dad's hammering is bothering them. It's so loud. It woke me up this morning."

The boy's mom looked at him for a moment. Then she walked over to the shed where his dad was.

"Honey, could you stop for the rest of the day?"

He stopped and looked down. "Fine." He dropped his hammer and put two hands up like he was surrendering to the police.

"You can find something else to do that isn't so loud," the boy's mom said.

The boy's dad came down the ladder. It shook with each step. After he got to the bottom, they heard the screen door to Tyler's house open and slam shut. Then they heard the high pitched scream of a girl. It echoed up and down the street like the boy's dad's hammer. It echoed off the shed and the trees around them.

The boy knew it must have been Tyler's sister. The boy looked at his mom, and she looked at his dad. They stood in silence. Then they heard Tyler's screen door open and slam shut again.

"Do you think that means she died?" the boy asked his mom.

"I don't know," she said.

He tried again to imagine what it looked like inside Tyler's house. What was Tyler doing? Was he crying and holding his mom's hand? Had he locked himself in his bedroom? Was he smashing glasses and plates on the floor?

No matter how hard he tried to understand and imagine, it didn't seem right. He didn't know how Tyler felt. He might never know. The boy's mom was standing right here, and tomorrow his dad would be hammering again.

About The Author

Devan Hawkins is a freelance writer from Massachusetts. His fiction has appeared in *In Shades* magazine and *Litro*. His writing about travel, books, and politics has appeared in a number of places including *The Los Angeles Times*, *The Islamic Monthly*, *CounterPunch*, and Matador Network. Outside of writing, Devan works in and teaches about public health.

About The Publisher

Story Shares is a nonprofit focused on supporting the millions of teens and adults who struggle with reading by creating a new shelf in the library specifically for them. The ever-growing collection features content that is compelling and culturally relevant for teens and adults, yet still readable at a range of lower reading levels.

Story Shares generates content by engaging deeply with writers, bringing together a community to create this new kind of book. With more intriguing and approachable stories to choose from, the teens and adults who have fallen behind are improving their skills and beginning to discover the joy of reading. For more information, visit storyshares.org.

Easy to Read. Hard to Put Down.

www.ingramcontent.com/pod-product-compliance
Lightning Source LLC
Chambersburg PA
CBHW071230170626
46809CB00005BA/2018